You Can't Catch Me!

ANNABEL COLLIS

Little, Brown and Company

Boston Toronto London

For Emma and Oliver

First U.S. Edition 1993
First published in Great Britain by
The Bodley Head Children's Books

Library of Congress Cataloguing-in-
Publication Data
Collis, Annabel.
    You can't catch me! / Annabel Collis.
    — 1st U.S. ed.
        p.   cm.
    Summary: While visiting the
playground with his brother and sister,
a young boy uses his imagination to
make the experience more exciting.
    ISBN 0-316-15237-4
    [1. Playground — Fiction. 2.
Imagination — Fiction. 3. Brothers and
sisters — Fiction.] I. Title.
PZ7.C6975Yo   1993
[E] — dc20   92-54486

Joy Street Books are published by Little,
Brown and Company (Inc.)
10 9 8 7 6 5 4 3 2 1

Printed in Hong Kong

My brother and sister are taking me to play
on the jungle gym. "Just hold on tight and
don't get lost!" they say.
But I tell them, "Monkey is taking me to a
real jungle — and you can't catch me!"

Once we climb this
rope ladder, Monkey and I will be...

sailing aboard a ship on
a stormy sea.

Here we go — now you can't catch me!

Eeek! The alligators are trying to snap us up!

But Monkey and I are clever as can be.

See, you can't catch me!

Swinging across the ocean I go...

Oh, no!

Quick, pull me up.
Don't be slow!

Look — Monkey knows the
way out of this place…

but all the wild animals want to chase.

Whee — they can't catch me!

Quick, let's slide. There's only room for four...

sorry, no more!

Phew! Hurray, we're free!

It's time to go home —
now you *can* catch me!